Wee Sing®
for
Christmas

by
Pamela Conn Beall
and
Susan Hagen Nipp

Illustrated
by
Nancy Klein

PRICE STERN SLOAN
Los Angeles

DEDICATION

To our friends everywhere —
We wish you a joyous Christmas.

Five Little Candles (Fingerplay), Born This Night, Where Is the Baby?, Bells Are Ringing, Merrily Caroling, Hear the Jingle Bells, Alfie the Elf, Reindeer Are Tapping, Down through the Chimney (Fingerplay), Copyright © 1984 by Susan Hagen Nipp. *Three Great Kings (Fingerplay), Three Little Christmas Trees (Fingerplay),* Copyright © 1984 by Pamela Conn Beall.

TABLE OF CONTENTS

Here Comes Santa Claus

Here We Come A-Caroling

HERE WE COME A-CAROLING

English

1. Here we come a-car-ol-ing A-mong the leaves so green;

Here we come a-wan-d'ring, So fair —— to be seen.

Refrain

Love and joy come to you, And to you glad Christ-mas

too; And God bless you and send —— you A hap-py New

Year, And God send you a hap-py New —— Year.

2. We are not daily beggars
   That beg from door to door,
   But we are neighbors' children
   Whom you have seen before.
   (Refrain)

3. God bless the master of this house,
   Likewise the mistress, too;
   And all the little children
   That 'round the table go.
   (Refrain)

4. And all your kin and kinsfolk
   That dwell both far and near,
   I wish you Merry Christmas
   And Happy New Year.
   (Refrain)

6

DECK THE HALLS

Welsh

1. Deck the halls with boughs of hol-ly, Fa, la, la, la, la, la, la, la, la. 'Tis the sea-son to be jol-ly, Fa, la, la, la, la, la, la, la, la. Don we now our gay ap-par-el, Fa, la, la, la, la, la, la, la, la. Troll the an-cient yule-tide car-ol, Fa, la, la, la, la, la, la, la, la.

2. See the blazing Yule before us ...
Strike the harp and join the chorus ...
Follow me in merry measure ...
While I tell of Yuletide treasure ...

3. Fast away the old year passes ...
Hail the new, ye lads and lasses ...
Sing we joyous all together ...
Heedless of the wind and weather ...

7

WE WISH YOU A MERRY CHRISTMAS

English

1. We wish you a mer-ry Christ-mas, We wish you a mer-ry Christ-mas, We wish you a mer-ry Christ-mas and a hap-py New Year.

Refrain Good tid-ings we bring to you and your Kin: We wish you a mer-ry Christ-mas and a hap-py New Year.

2. Oh, bring us some figgy pudding,
   Oh, bring us some figgy pudding,
   Oh, bring us some figgy pudding,
   And bring it right here.
3. We won't go until we get some,
   (3 times)
   So bring it right here.
4. We all like our figgy pudding,
   (3 times)
   With all its good cheer.
5. We wish you a Merry Christmas,
   (3 times)
   And a Happy New Year.
   (Refrain)

O CHRISTMAS TREE

German

O Christ-mas tree, O Christ-mas tree, How ev-er-green your branch-es! O Christ-mas tree, O Christ-mas tree, How ev-er-green your branch-es! They're green when sum-mer days are bright, They're green when win-ter snow is white, O Christ-mas tree, O Christ-mas tree, How ev-er-green your branch-es!

JINGLE BELLS

James Pierpont

1. Dash-ing through the snow In a one horse o - pen

sleigh, O'er the fields we go, Laugh-ing all the way;

Bells on bob-tails ring, Mak-ing spir-its bright, What

fun it is to ride and sing a sleigh-ing song to-night.

(Refrain)

Jin-gle bells! Jin-gle bells! Jin-gle all the way!

Oh, what fun it is to ride in a one horse o-pen sleigh:-

Jin-gle bells! Jin-gle bells! Jin-gle all the way!

Oh, what fun it is to ride in a one horse o-pen sleigh

2. A day or two ago
   I thought I'd take a ride,
   And soon Miss Fannie Bright
   Was seated by my side;
   The horse was lean and lank,
   Misfortune seemed his lot,
   He got into a drifted bank,
   And we, we got upsot.
      (Refrain)
3. Now the ground is white,
   Go it while you're young,
   Take the girls tonight,
   And sing this sleighing song.
   Just get a bobtailed bay,
   Two-forty for his speed,
   Then hitch him to an open sleigh,
   And crack! you'll take the lead.
      (Refrain)

Suggestion: For young children, give
each child a bell of some type. Gallop
with bells on verse. Stop and ring
bells on refrain.

*Easier chords for guitar. (To sound in same key as piano, guitar put capo on first fret.)

11

THE TWELVE DAYS OF CHRISTMAS

1. On the first day of Christ-mas, my true love sent to me A par-tridge—in a pear tree

2. On the sec-ond
3. On the third } day of Christ-mas, my true love sent to me
4. On the fourth

Two tur-tle doves,
Three French hens, } And a par-tridge—in a pear tree
Four cal-ling birds,

5. On the fifth day of Christ-mas, my true love sent to me

Five gold-en rings! Four—cal-ling birds, Three French hens,

Two—tur-tle doves, And a par-tridge—in a pear tree

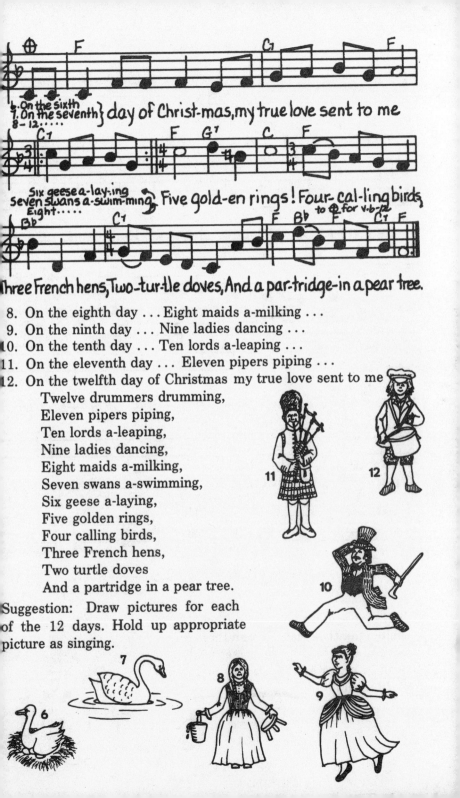

6. On the sixth
7. On the seventh } day of Christ-mas, my true love sent to me

Six geese a-lay-ing
Seven swans a-swim-ming } Five gold-en rings! Four cal-ling birds,
Eight.....

Three French hens, Two tur-tle doves, And a par-tridge in a pear tree.

8. On the eighth day . . . Eight maids a-milking . . .
9. On the ninth day . . . Nine ladies dancing . . .
10. On the tenth day . . . Ten lords a-leaping . . .
11. On the eleventh day . . . Eleven pipers piping . . .
12. On the twelfth day of Christmas my true love sent to me
     Twelve drummers drumming,
     Eleven pipers piping,
     Ten lords a-leaping,
     Nine ladies dancing,
     Eight maids a-milking,
     Seven swans a-swimming,
     Six geese a-laying,
     Five golden rings,
     Four calling birds,
     Three French hens,
     Two turtle doves
     And a partridge in a pear tree.

Suggestion: Draw pictures for each
of the 12 days. Hold up appropriate
picture as singing.

CAPO 2

THE FIRST NOEL

English

1. The — first — No — el the — an-gel did say, was to cer-tain poor shep-herds in fields as they lay; In — fields — where — they lay — Keep-ing their sheep, On a cold win-ter's night — that was — so deep.

Refrain

No — el, — No — el, No — el, No-el, Born is the King — of Is — ra – el.

2. They look-ed up and saw a star
   Shining in the East, beyond them far,
   And to the earth it gave great light,
   And so it continued both day and night.
   (Refrain)

JOY TO THE WORLD

Isaac Watts   1719   Lowell Mason   1839

1. Joy to the world, the Lord is come, Let earth receive her King,— Let ev—'ry —heart —prepare —Him— room,— And heav'n and na-ture— sing, And —heav'n and na-ture — sing, And —heav'n,— and heav'n —— and na-ture sing.

2. Joy to the earth, the Savior reigns,
   Let men their songs employ,
   While fields and floods, rocks, hills and plains
   Repeat the sounding joy, Repeat the sounding joy,
   Repeat, repeat the sounding joy.

3. He rules the world with truth and grace,
   And makes the nations prove
   The glories of His righteousness,
   And wonders of His love,
   And wonders of His love,
   And wonders, and wonders of His love.

15

WE THREE KINGS

J.H.H.   *John H. Hopkins* 1857

We three Kings of Or- i- ent are, Bear-ing

gifts we tra-verse a-far, Field and foun- tain,

moor and moun—tain, Fol-low-ing yon-der star.

Refrain

O—— star of won-der, star of night, Star with

roy-al beau-ty bright, West- ward lead-ing

still pro-ceed-ing, Guide us to thy per-fect light.

O COME, ALL YE FAITHFUL

J.F.W.

English

1. O come, all ye faith-ful, Joy-ful and tri-um-phant, O come ye, O come — ye to Beth — le-hem; Come and be-hold Him, Born the King of An — gels, O come let us a-dore Him, O come let us a-dore Him, O come let us a-dore Him, — Christ — the Lord.

2. Sing, choirs of angels,
   Sing in exultation,
   Sing, all ye citizens of heav'n above;
   Glory to God In the highest,
   O come let us adore Him . . .

3. Yea, Lord, we greet Thee,
   Born this happy morning;
   Jesus, to Thee be all glory giv'n,
   Word of the Father Now in flesh appearing,
   O come let us adore Him . . .

Suggestion: For a group, begin with only a few voices on "O come let us adore Him". Add more voices the second time and all voices the third.

17

O LITTLE TOWN OF BETHLEHEM

Phillips Brooks   19th C.   *Lewis H. Redner   19th C.*

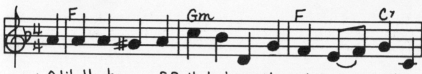

1. O lit-tle town of Beth-le-hem, How still we—see thee

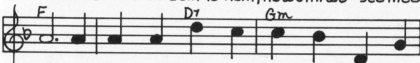

lie, A-bove thy deep and dream-less sleep The

si-lent — stars go by, Yet in thy dark streets

shin-eth The ev-er-last-ing Light, The hopes and

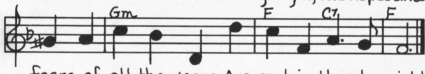

fears of all the years Are met in thee to-night.

2. For Christ is born of Mary,
   And gathered all above,
   While mortals sleep, the angels keep
   Their watch of wond'ring love.
   O morning stars together
   Proclaim the holy birth,
   And praises sing to God the King,
   And peace to men on earth.

AWAY IN A MANGER

German

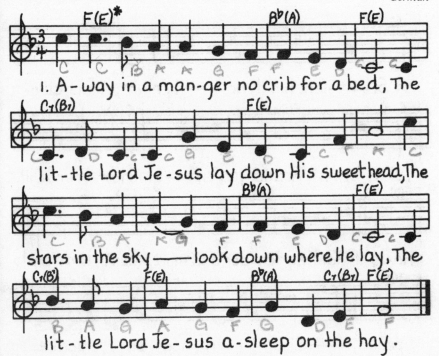

1. A-way in a man-ger no crib for a bed, The
lit-tle Lord Je-sus lay down His sweet head, The
stars in the sky —— look down where He lay, The
lit-tle Lord Je-sus a-sleep on the hay.

2. The cattle are lowing, the Baby awakes,
   But little Lord Jesus, no crying he makes,
   I love Thee, Lord Jesus, look down from the sky,
   And stay by my cradle till morning is nigh.

3. Be near me, Lord Jesus, I ask Thee to stay
   Close by me forever, and love me, I pray,
   Bless all the dear children in Thy tender care,
   And take us to heaven to live with Thee there.

*Easier chords for guitar. (To sound in same key as piano, guitar put capo on first fret.)

SILENT NIGHT

Joseph Mohr 1818 *Franz Gruber 1818*

1. Silent night, Holy night, All is calm, All is bright, 'Round yon Virgin, Mother and Child, Holy infant so tender and mild, Sleep in heavenly peace, Sleep in heavenly peace.

2. Silent night, Holy night,
   Shepherds quake at the sight,
   Glories stream from heaven afar,
   Heav'nly hosts sing Alleluia,
   Christ, the Savior, is born,
   Christ, the Savior, is born.

3. Silent night, Holy night,
   Son of God, love's pure light,
   Radiant beams from Thy holy face,
   With the dawn of redeeming grace,
   Jesus, Lord at Thy birth,
   Jesus, Lord at Thy birth.

*Easier chords for guitar. (To sound in same key as piano, guitar put capo on third fret.)

20

Birthday of a King

BIRTHDAY OF A KING

W.H.N.

W.H. Neidlinger

1.In the lit-tle vil-lage of Beth-le-hem There lay a child one day, And the sky was bright with a ho-ly light O'er the place where Je-sus lay.

Refrain

Al-le-lu-ia! O how the an-gels sang, Al-le-lu-ia! How it rang! And the sky was bright with a ho-ly light, 'Twas the birth-day of a King!

2. 'Twas a humble birthplace, but oh, how much
   God gave to us that day,
   From a manger bed, what a path hath led,
   What a perfect holy way.
       (Refrain)

FUM, FUM, FUM

Spanish (Catalan) Carol

1. On De-cem-ber five and twen-ty, fum, fum, fum. On De-cem-ber five and twen-ty, fum, fum, fum. He is born for love of us, The Son of God, The Son of God; He is born of Vir-gin Ma-ry, On this night so cold and drear-y, fum, fum, fum.

2. Little birds out in the wood,
   Sing fum, fum, fum.
   Little birds out in the wood,
   Sing fum, fum, fum.
   All your fledglings on the bough,
   O leave them now, O leave them now.
   Make a soft and downy nest
   So the newborn Babe may rest,
   Sing fum, fum, fum.

3. Little stars up in the sky,
   Sing fum, fum, fum.
   Little stars up in the sky,
   Sing fum, fum, fum.
   See the little Jesus crying,
   Don't you cry, O don't you cry,
   Fill the night with twinkling light,
   Oh wondrous stars that shine so bright,
   Sing fum, fum, fum.

'TWAS IN THE MOON OF WINTERTIME

Original words in Huron Indian
by Father Jean de Brebeuf   1593-1649

Traditional French

'Twas in the moon of win-ter-time When all the birds had fled, That might-y Git-chi Man-i-tou Sent an-gel choirs in-stead. Be-fore their light the stars grew dim, And wan-d'ring hun-ters heard the hymn:——

Refrain

"Je-sus your King is born, Je-sus is born, In ex-cel-sis glo-ri-a!"

2. Within a lodge of broken bark
   The tender Babe was found,
   A ragged robe of rabbit skin
   Enwrapped His beauty 'round.
   And as the hunter braves drew nigh,
   The angel song rang loud and high:
      (Refrain)
3. The earliest moon of wintertime
   Is not so round and fair,
   As was the ring of glory on
   The helpless Infant there,
   While Chiefs from far before Him knelt
   With gifts of fox and beaver pelt.
      (Refrain)
4. O children of the forest free,
   O sons of Manitou,
   The Holy Child of earth and Heav'n
   Is born today for you.
   Come, kneel before the radiant Boy
   Who brings you beauty, peace and joy.
      (Refrain)

The "Huron Carol" was the first Canadian Christmas carol, perhaps the first carol of the New World. Father Jean de Brebeuf, a Jesuit missionary who worked among the Huron Indians in Canada, wrote the original Indian words to tell the Christmas story in a language the Indians could understand. He used the tune of an old French carol.

ANGEL BAND

Spiritual

There was one, there were two, there were three lit-tle

an-gels, There were four, there were five, there were six lit-tle

an-gels, There were sev-en, there were eight, there were

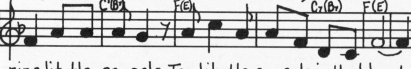

nine lit-tle an-gels, Ten lit-tle an-gels in that band.—

Oh, was-n't that a band, Christ-mas morn —ing, Christ-mas

*Easier chords for guitar. (To sound in same key as piano, guitar put capo on first fret.)

morn—ing, Christ-mas morn—ing, Was-n't that a

band, Christ-mas morn—ing, Christ-mas morn-ing soon.

Suggestion: Ten children stand in a row, numbered from one to ten. Each child has a rhythm instrument (triangle, bells, finger cymbals, tambourine, etc.). The child begins to sing and play when his number is sung and continues playing until song ends.

FIVE LITTLE CANDLES
(Fingerplay)

Susan Nipp

Five little candles burning so bright,
    (hold up   (wiggle fingers)
    five fingers)

The first one said, "We make great light!"
    (hold up   (arms up)
    one finger)

The second one said, "The child is born."
    (hold up   (rock baby)
    two fingers)

The third one said, "Our light will adorn."
    (hold up   (arms out in front,
    three fingers)   palms up)

The fourth one said, "We shine for Him."
    (hold up   (palms forward at sides
    four fingers)   of face, fingers spread)

The fifth one said, "Let's not be dim."
    (hold up   (cover pointer finger
    five fingers)   with other hand)

So they stood very tall and glowed very bright,
    (stand tall)   (arms up)

And the Christ child smiled that very night.
    (smile, hands around face)

MARCH OF THE KINGS

French   13th C.

Three great Kings I met at ear-ly morn, With
all their ret-i-nue were slow-ly march-ing,
Three great Kings I met at ear-ly morn, Were
on their way to meet the new-ly born, With
gifts of gold brought from far a-way, And
val-iant war-riors to guard the king-ly treas-ure, With
gifts of gold brought from far a-way, And
shields all shin-ing in their bright ar-ray.

THREE GREAT KINGS
(Fingerplay)

Pam Beall

Three great kings on a cold winter's night
    (hold up three fingers) (hug self, shivering)

Found the baby Jesus, guided by the light.
    (rock arms)   (point to sky)

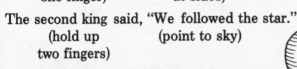

The first king said, "We've come so far."
    (hold up   (arms out
    one finger)   at sides)

The second king said, "We followed the star."
    (hold up   (point to sky)
    two fingers)

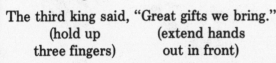

The third king said, "Great gifts we bring."
    (hold up   (extend hands
    three fingers)   out in front)

And together they said, "Great praises we sing."
    (hold up   (hands around mouth)
    three fingers)

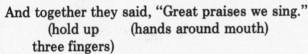

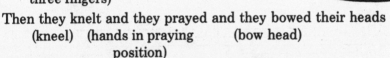

Then they knelt and they prayed and they bowed their heads
    (kneel)   (hands in praying   (bow head)
                position)

As they worshipped baby Jesus in His manger bed.
    (sit on heels, extend arms forward to floor, bow head)

Suggestion: Dramatization for young children
Narrators (group of children)
Narrate entire poem except words spoken by three kings. Narrators
do not do any motions.

Three Kings (three children dressed as kings) enter as first three
lines are being narrated.
1st King—Speaks quoted words on line 3, doing motions
2nd King—line 4
3rd King—line 5
All 3 Kings—quoted words and motions, line 6

As last two lines are being narrated, the three kings do motions.

WIND THROUGH THE OLIVE TREES

Traditional

1. Wind through the ol-ive trees soft-ly did blow

'Round lit-tle Beth-le-hem, long, long a-go.

2. Sheep on the hillside lay whiter than snow,
   Shepherds were watching them, long, long ago.
3. Then from the starry skies angels bent low,
   Singing their songs of joy, long, long ago.
4. For in a manger bed long, long ago,
   Christ came to Bethlehem, long, long, ago.

JOSEPH DEAREST, JOSEPH MINE

German   14th C.

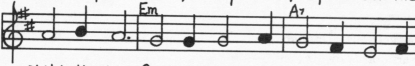

1. Jo-seph dear-est, Jo-seph mine, Help me rock the

Child di-vine, God re-ward thee and all thine in

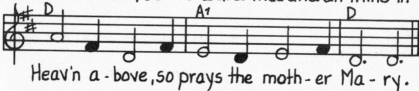

Heav'n a-bove, so prays the moth-er Ma-ry.

2. Gladly, Mary, lady mine,
   I'll help rock the Child divine,
   God's own light on both us shine
   In Heav'n above, so prays the Mother Mary.

BORN THIS NIGHT

S.N.

Susan Nipp

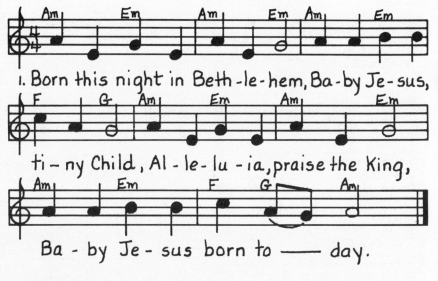

1. Born this night in Beth-le-hem, Ba-by Je-sus,

ti - ny Child, Al - le - lu - ia, praise the King,

Ba - by Je - sus born to —— day.

(last measure)

2. Kneel before Him as He sleeps,
   Baby Jesus, tiny child,
   Al-le-lu-ia, praise the King,
   Baby Jesus born today.
3. Worship Him, our Savior's come,
   Baby Jesus, tiny child,
   Al-le-lu-ia, praise the King,
   Baby Jesus born today.

Suggestions: 1. Use bells, piano or recorder for repeated pattern of ostinato. 2. Use finger cymbals or triangle on beats one and three throughout.

THE LITTLE DRUMMER BOY

K.D., H.O., H.S.   *Katherine Davis, Henry Onorati, Harry Simeone*

1. Come, they told me, (Pa-rum-pum-pum-pum) —

A new-born King to see; (Pa-rum-pum-pum-pum) —

Our fin-est gifts we bring, (Pa-rum-pum-pum-pum) —

To lay be-fore the King, (Pa-rum-pum-pum-pum,

rum-pum-pum-pum, rum-pum-pum-pum) — So to

hon-or Him (Pa-rum-pum-pum-pum) — When — we come.

2. Little Baby, (Pa-rum-pum-pum-pum)
   I am a poor boy, too, (Pa-rum-pum-pum-pum)
   I have no gift to bring (Pa-rum-pum-pum-pum)
   That's fit to give our King. (Pa-rum-pum-pum-pum, rum-pum-
      pum-pum, rum-pum-pum-pum)
   Shall I play for You (Pa-rum-pum-pum-pum)
   On my drum?
3. Mary nodded; (Pa-rum-pum-pum-pum)
   The ox and lamb kept time; (Pa-rum-pum-pum-pum)
   I played my drum for Him; (Pa-rum-pum-pum-pum)
   I played my best for Him. (Pa-rum-pum-pum-pum, rum-pum-
      pum-pum, rum-pum-pum-pum)
   Then He smiled at me, (Pa-rum-pum-pum-pum)
   Me and my drum.

WHERE IS THE BABY?

S.N.   *Susan Nipp*

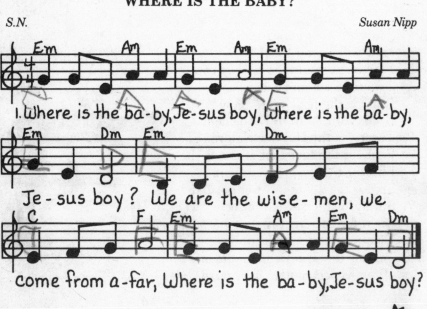

1. Where is the ba-by, Je-sus boy, Where is the ba-by, Je-sus boy? We are the wise-men, we come from a-far, Where is the ba-by, Je-sus boy?

2. We've come to worship Jesus boy,
   We've come to worship Jesus boy,
   We are the wise men, we come from afar,
   We've come to worship Jesus boy.
3. He is our Savior, Jesus boy . . .
4. Where is the baby, Jesus boy . . .

CHILDREN, GO WHERE I SEND THEE

Spiritual

1. Children, go where I send thee, How shall I send thee? I'm gonna send thee—one by one, One for the little bitty Baby born, born —— born in Bethlehem.

2. Children, go where I send thee,
   How will I send thee?
   I'm gonna send thee two by two,
   Two for Paul and Silas,
   One for the little bitty Baby,
   Born, born, born in Bethlehem.
3. Three for the Hebrew children . . .
4. Four for the four that stood at the door . . .
5. Five for the gospel preachers . . .
6. Six for the six that never got fixed . . .
7. Seven for the seven that never went to Heaven . . .
8. Eight for the eight that stood at the gate . . .
9. Nine for the nine that dressed so fine . . .
10. Ten for the Ten Commandments . . .
    (Verses accumulate in reverse order.)

WHAT CHILD IS THIS?

William C. Dix   1865   *Old English "Greensleeves"   17th C.*

What Child is this — Who, laid to rest — On
Ma-ry's lap, — is sleep-ing? Whom an-gels greet — with
an-thems sweet — While shep-herds watch — are keep-ing?

Refrain

This, this — is Christ the King, — Whom
shep-herds guard — and an-gels sing: Haste, haste — to
bring Him laud, — The Babe, — The Son — of Ma-ry!

2. So bring Him incense, gold and myrrh,
   Come peasant, king to own Him,
   The King of kings salvation brings,
   Let loving hearts enthrone Him.
   (Refrain)

BELLS ARE RINGING

S.N.

Susan Nipp

Bells are ring-ing, Bells are ring-ing, Ba-by Je-sus born to-day,

Bells are ring-ing, Bells are ring-ing, Ba-by Je-sus born to-day.

Cel-e-brate His birth in Beth-le-hem, Cel-e-brate His birth with joy,

Bells are ring-ing, Bells are ring-ing, Ba-by Je-sus born to-day.

Ostinato

Bells   Triangle   Finger cymbals

Suggestion: Use bells, triangle and finger cymbals for a two measure introduction. Continue ostinato throughout the song and add two measures after singing is completed. The bell part could also be played on the piano.

O COME, LITTLE CHILDREN

Christoph von Schmidt   *J.A.P. Schulz*   *18th C.*

1. O come, lit-tle child-ren, O come, one and all,

O come to the man-ger in Beth-le-hem's stall,

And see the Lord Je-sus a-sleep in the hay,

The lit-tle Lord Je-sus was born Christ-mas Day.

2. He lies in the manger,
   The hay is His bed,
   The star, high in heaven,
   Shines over His head,
   And Mary and Joseph
   Look down on the boy,
   While shepherds and wise men
   Kneel down in their joy.

3. Now "Glory to God!" comes
   The song from on high,
   And "Peace for all mankind!"
   We sing in reply,
   Then come, little children,
   Be happy and gay,
   For Jesus, the Christ Child,
   Was born Christmas Day.

Suggestion: Children act out manger scene as other children gather around. Add shepherds and wise men on Verse 2, angels on Verse 3.

PAT-A-PAN

B.M.

Bernard de la Monnoye 1700

1. Wil-lie, take your lit-tle drum; Rob-in, bring your flute and come. We'll be joy-ous as you play, Tu-re-lu-re-lu, Pat-a-pat-a-pan; We'll be joy-ous as you play, on a mer-ry — Christ-mas day.

2. When the men of olden days
   Gave the King of Kings their praise,
   They had pipes on which to play
   Tu-re-lu-re-lu, pat-a-pat-a-pan,
   They had drums on which to play,
   Full of joy on Christmas Day.

3. God and man this day become
   Joined as one with flute and drum.
   Let the happy tune play on,
   Tu-re-lu-re-lu, pat-a-pat-a-pan,
   Flute and drum together play
   As we sing on Christmas Day.

Suggestion: Use rhythm instruments throughout. On "tu-re-lu-re-lu," use kazoos or recorders. On "pat-a-pat-a-pan," use drums and sticks.

STILL, STILL, STILL

Austrian 19th C.

Still, still,—still, The lit-tle—Je-sus sleeps.

Ten-der-ly His moth-er holds Him,

Near her heart she gent-ly folds Him,

Still, still,—still, The lit-tle—Je-sus sleeps.

COVENTRY CAROL

Robert Croo 1543 *English 1591*

1. Lul-ly, lul-lay, Thou lit-tle, ti-ny Child,

By, by, lul-ly, lul-lay; Lul-lay Thou lit-tle,

ti-ny Child, By, by, lul-ly, lul-lay.

GO TELL IT ON THE MOUNTAIN

Spiritual

Go tell it on the moun-tain, O-ver the hills and ev——'ry——where, Go tell it on the moun-tain, Our heav'n-ly Lord —— is born.

1. While shep-herds kept their watch-ing O'er si-lent flocks by night, Be-hold through-out the heav-ens There shone a ho-ly light,——

(Refrain)

2. The shepherds feared and trembled When lo! above the earth,
   Rang out the angel chorus That hailed our Savior's birth.
   (Refrain)

3. Down in a lowly manger Our humble Christ was born,
   And God sent us salvation That blessed Christmas morn.
   (Refrain)

*Easier chords for guitar. (To sound in same key as piano, guitar put capo on first fret.)

THE FRIENDLY BEASTS

Robert Davis   *French   12th C.*

1. Je-sus our Broth-er, kind and good, Was

hum-bly born in a sta-ble rude, The friend-ly beasts a-

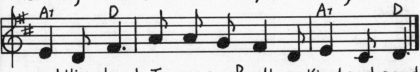

round Him stood, Je-sus our Broth-er, kind and good.

2. "I," said the donkey, shaggy and brown,
   "I carried His mother up hill and down,
   I carried His mother to Bethlehem town.
   I," said the donkey, shaggy and brown.

3. "I," said the cow all white and red,
   "I gave Him my manger for His bed,
   I gave Him my hay to pillow His head.
   I," said the cow all white and red.

4. "I," said the sheep with curly horn,
   "I gave Him my wool for His blanket warm,
   He wore my coat on Christmas morn.
   I," said the sheep with curly horn.

5. "I," said the dove from rafters high,
   "I cooed Him to sleep that He should not cry,
   We cooed Him to sleep, my mate and I.
   I," said the dove from rafters high.

6. Thus ev'ry beast by some good spell,
   In the stable dark was glad to tell
   Of the gift he gave Emmanuel.
   The gift he gave Emmanuel.

Suggestion: For a group, select solos for Verses 2-5. Dress as, or
              hold pictures of, the animal represented.

ROCKING

Czech Carol

1. Little Jesus, sweetly sleep, do not stir,
We will lend you a coat of fur,
We will rock you, rock you, rock you,
We will rock you, rock you, rock you,
See the fur to keep you warm,
Snugly 'round your tiny form.

2. Mary's little baby, sleep, sweetly sleep,
Sleep in comfort, slumber deep,
We will rock you, rock you, rock you,
We will rock you, rock you, rock you,
We will serve you all we can,
Darling, darling little man.

Translated by A.F. Dearmer: from the Oxford Book of Carols by permission of the Oxford University Press.

Here Comes Santa Claus

HERE COMES SANTA CLAUS

Autry/Haldeman   *Gene Autry, Oakley Haldeman*

Here comes San-ta Claus, Here comes San-ta Claus

Right down San-ta Claus lane. Vix-en and Blitz-en and

All his rein-deer are pul-ling on the rein.

Bells are ring-ing, Chil-dren sing-ing

All is mer-ry and bright, Hang your stock-ings and

say your pray'rs, 'Cause San-ta Claus comes to-night

2. Here comes Santa Claus, Here comes Santa Claus
   Right down Santa Claus Lane.
   He's got a bag that is filled with toys
   For the boys and girls again.
   Hear those sleigh bells jingle jangle,
   What a beautiful sight.
   Jump in bed, cover up your head,
   'Cause Santa Claus comes tonight.

3. Here comes Santa Claus, Here comes Santa Claus
   Right down Santa Claus Lane.
   He doesn't care if you're rich or poor
   For he loves you just the same.
   Santa knows that we're God's children;
   That makes ev'rything right.
   Fill your hearts with a Christmas cheer,
   'Cause Santa Claus comes tonight.

4. Here comes Santa Claus, Here comes Santa Claus
   Right down Santa Claus Lane.
   He'll come around when the chimes ring out;
   Then it's Christmas morn again.
   Peace on earth will come to all
   If we just follow the light.
   Let's give thanks to the Lord above,
   'Cause Santa Claus comes tonight.

THE CHIMNEY
(Fingerplay)

Here is the chimney,
    (make a fist)

Here is the top,
    (other hand over fist)

Open the lid,
    (remove hand)

Out Santa will pop!
    (pop up thumb)

UP ON THE HOUSETOP

Traditional

1. Up on the house top rein-deer pause,

Out jumps good old San - ta Claus;

Down through the chim - ney with lots of toys,

All for the lit - tle ones, Christ-mas joys.

Refrain

Ho, ho, ho! Who would - nt go!

Ho, ho, ho! Who would - nt go!

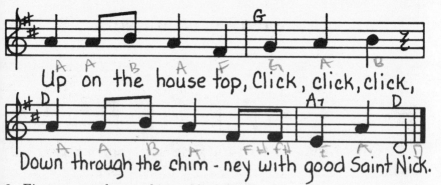

Up on the house top, Click, click, click,
Down through the chim - ney with good Saint Nick.

2. First comes the stocking of little Nell;
   Oh, dear Santa, fill it well;
   Give her a dolly that laughs and cries,
   One that can open and shut its eyes.
       (Refrain)

3. Look in the stocking of little Will;
   Oh, just see what a glorious fill!
   Here is a hammer and lots of tacks,
   Whistle and ball and a whip that cracks.
       (Refrain)

Suggestion: For sound effects: "click, click,
click" —click tongue and/or snap fingers;
"whip that cracks"—clap hands right after
singing "cracks"

WHEN SANTA COMES
(Fingerplay)

When Santa comes to our house,
    (hands form pointed roof)

I would like to peek,
    (peek through fingers)

But I know he'll never come
    (shake head no)

Until I'm fast asleep.
    (rest head on hands)

CHRISTMAS IS COMING
(Round)

English

1. Christ-mas is com-ing, The goose is get-ting fat,

Please to put a pen-ny in the old man's —— hat,

Please to put a pen-ny in the old man's hat.

2. If you have no penny,
   a ha'penny will do,
   If you have no ha'penny,
   then God bless you,
   If you have no ha'penny,
   then God bless you.

MERRILY CAROLING
(Round)

S.N.

Susan Nipp

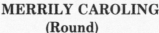

Mer-ri-ly, car-ol-ing, Sing-ing joy for Christ-mas,

Hap-pi-ly, cheer-ful-ly, Sing-ing songs of joy.

RING, RING, RING THE BELLS
(Round/Tune: Row, Row, Row Your Boat)

Traditional

Ring, ring, ring the bells, Ring them loud and clear, —— To

tell the chil-dren ev-'ry-where That Christ-mas time is here.——

LITTLE BELLS OF CHRISTMAS

English

The lit-tle bells of Christ-mas say,

Ding, dong, ding, dong, dong, The lit-tle bells of

Christ-mas say, Ding, ding, dong.

Suggestion: 1. Use all types of bells and ringing instruments for rhythmic accompaniment.
2. May be sung as a round.

49

SANTA CLAUS IS COMING
(Round)

S.N.   *Traditional*

San-ta Claus is com-ing, Christ-mas is near,

Hang all the stock-ings, we can't wait 'til he's here.

CHRISTMAS BELLS
(Round)

Traditional

Ring, ring, the joy bells are ring-ing, the

chil-dren are sing-ing, For Christ-mas is here.

Bells

Suggestion: Play bells or
piano repeatedly for ostinato.

HEAR THE JINGLE BELLS

S.N.

Susan Nipp

Hear the jin-gle, jin-gle, jin-gle, Hear the jin-gle bells,

Ring-ing light-ly, ring-ing bright-ly, Hear the jin-gle bells.

Ostinato

Jin-gle, jin-gle, Ring those bells!

Suggestion: 1. Can be sung in three parts:
   Group 1 sings verse.
   Group 2 sings "Jingle, jingle" repeatedly.
   Group 3 sings "Ring those bells" repeatedly.
2. Ostinato can be played with tone bells or on piano.

FIVE LITTLE BELLS
(Fingerplay)

Unknown

Five little bells hanging in a row,
   (hold up five fingers)
The first one said, "Ring me slow."
   (move thumb slowly)
The second one said, "Ring me fast!"
   (move index finger quickly)
The third one said, "Ring me last."
   (move middle finger)
The fourth one said, "I'm like a chime."
   (move ring finger)
The fifth one said, "Ring us all at Christmas time."
   (wiggle all five fingers)

CHUBBY LITTLE SNOWMAN
(Fingerplay)

Unknown

A chubby little snowman
    (arms make fat tummy)
Had a carrot nose.
    (fist out in front of nose)
Along came a bunny,
    (hold up two fingers, hop hand)
And what do you suppose?
    (shake pointer finger)
That hungry little bunny,
    (rub tummy)
Looking for his lunch,
    (shade eyes, look around)
Ate the snowman's carrot nose,
    (fist out in front of nose)
Nibble, nibble, crunch!
    (open and close   (grab nose with fist
        fist twice)   moving toward nose)

THREE LITTLE CHRISTMAS TREES
(Fingerplay)

Pam Beall

Three little Christmas trees standing all alone,
    (hold up three fingers)

Their hearts were very sad 'cause they hadn't found a home.
    (hands over heart, sad face) (fingertips form pointed roof)

Then "CHOP" went the ax, and down fell a tree,
    (right hand chop   (palms together
        left forearm)   lean to side)
And off it went with a happy family.
    (bounce pointer finger   (smile with index fingers
        from left to right)   at corners of mouth)

Two little Christmas trees ...
One little Christmas tree ...

No little Christmas trees standing all alone,
    (pointer finger and thumb make a zero)
Their hearts were very happy
    (hands over heart)
'Cause they all had found a home.
    (fingertips form pointed roof)

CHRISTMAS DAY

Swedish

Christ-mas day will soon be here and I can hard-ly wait!

Christ-mas day will soon be here and I can hard-ly wait!

San-ta will be com-ing, Soon he will be com-ing,

Christ-mas day will soon be here and I can hard-ly wait!

Suggestion:
1. Use rhythm sticks and bells. Rhythm sticks play first eight measures, bells play next four, both groups play last four measures.
2. Circle game:
   Form circle, children holding hands.
   Measures 1- 4 - circle left
             5- 8 - circle right
             9-10 - four steps in
            11-12 - four steps out
            13-16 - circle left

MUST BE SANTA

H.M./B.F.

Hal Moore   Bill Fredricks

1. Who's got a beard that's long and white?

San-ta's got a beard that's long and white.

Who comes a-round on a spe-cial night?

San-ta comes a-round on a spe-cial night.

Spe - cial night, beard that's white,

Must be San - ta, Must be San - ta,

Must be San - ta, San - ta Claus.

Words and Music by Hal Moore and Bill Fredricks TRO—© Copyright 1960 Hollis Music, Inc., New York, N.Y. Used by Permission

2. Who's got boots and a suit of red?
Santa's got boots and a suit of red.
Who wears a long cap on his head?
Santa wears a long cap on his head.
Cap on head, suit that's red,
Special night, beard that's white,
(Chorus)

3. Who's got a great big cherry nose?
Santa's got a great big cherry nose.
Who laughs this way, "Ho, ho, ho?"
Santa laughs this way, "Ho, ho, ho."
Ho, ho, ho, cherry nose,
Cap on head, suit that's red,
Special night, beard that's white,
(Chorus)

4. Who very soon will come our way?
Santa very soon will come our way.
Eight little reindeer pull his sleigh,
Santa's little reindeer pull his sleigh.
Reindeer sleigh, come our way,
Ho, ho, ho, cherry nose,
Cap on head, suit that's red,
Special night, beard that's white,
(Chorus)

WE WISH YOU A MERRY CHRISTMAS
(Singing Game for Young Children)

Chorus: We wish you a Merry Christmas,
We wish you a Merry Christmas,
We wish you a Merry Christmas,
And a Happy New Year.

Verse 1:   Let's all do a little clapping,
Let's all do a little clapping,
Let's all do a little clapping,
And spread Christmas cheer.

Verse 2:   . . . jumping . . .

Verse 3:   . . . twirling . . .

Suggestion: On chorus, join hands and ring around circle. On verses, stand still and do motions. Repeat chorus after each verse. Add your own verses.

ALFIE THE ELF

S.N./P.B.   *Susan Nipp*

Al-fie the elf was San-ta's help-er, Al-fie the elf just

loved to try, But when he worked for dear old San-ta,

Al-fie the elf could on-ly cry, "Oh!" when he stubbed his toe,

"Umm," when he ham-mered his thumb, "Gee!" when he

banged his knee, "Boy!" when he broke a toy, —

Al-fie the elf was so dis-cour-aged, "Help me, please San-ta

56

RING THOSE BELLS
(Tune: Jimmy Crack Corn)

S.N.

Traditional

1. Ring those bells and turn a-round,

Ring those bells and turn a-round,

Ring those bells and turn a-round for

Christ-mas time has come.

2. Ring those bells and stomp your feet . . .
3. Ring those bells and jump up high . . .

Make up your own additional verses.

Suggestion: Use any type of bell or ringing instrument on "Ring Those Bells." (Wrist bells can be made by sliding jingle bells onto thick yarn and tying onto wrist.)

REINDEER ARE TAPPING

S.N.

Susan Nipp

Rein-deer are tap-ping on the roof-top, and while they're tap-ping

San-ta is get-ting all the pack-a-ges for you and me,

own through the chim-ney with his knap-sack, and when the job is

fin-ished, Dear San-ta and his rein-deer fly a-way.

Ostinato

tap-ping, tap-ping, tap-ping, tap-ping, (Glissando at end)

Suggestion:
1. Use rhythm sticks and wood blocks for a constant tapping sound.
2. Use bells and/or voices for the ostinato (played continuously through song).
3. When using bells, play a glissando at end (slide mallet over bells quickly from low to high).

59

JOLLY OLD ST. NICHOLAS

U.S.A.

1. Jol-ly old St. Nich-o-las, Lean your ear this way
(make arms be a fat tummy) (hand cup ear)

Don't you tell a sin-gle soul what I'm going to say
(shake pointer finger) (hands cup mouth)

Christ-mas Eve will soon be here, Now you dear old man
(point to wrist watch) (make arms be a fat tummy)

Whis-per what you'll bring to me, Tell me if you can.
(hands cup mouth) (hand cup ear)

2. When the clock is striking twelve,
     (hands praying position, rock back and forth)
   When I'm fast asleep,
     (rest head on hands)
   Down the chimney with your pack,
     (swoop arm downward, throw pack over shoulder)
   Softly you will creep,
     (creep hands)
   All the stockings you will find
     (point to own stockings)
   Hanging in a row;
     (mimic hanging stockings)
   Mine will be the shortest one,
     (point to self,
       show short measurement)
   You'll be sure to know.
     (shake pointer finger)

Johnny wants a pair of skates,
   (hands together, palms down, push forward)
Susie needs a sled,
   (make swooping motion downward)
Nelly wants a story book,
   (hands together, palms facing you)
One she hasn't read,
   (shake head side to side)
As for me, I hardly know,
   (point to self, shake head)
So I'll go to rest;
   (rest head on hands)
Choose for me, dear Santa Claus,
   (point to self)
What you think is best.
   (shrug shoulders, throw hands out to sides)

TAPPING
(Tune: Twinkle, Twinkle, Little Star)

S.N.   *Traditional*

Tap-ping, tap-ping, lit-tle elf, As you work up-on your shelf,

Work-ing hard to make some toys, All for lit-tle girls and boys,

Tap-ping, tap-ping, lit-tle elf, As you work up-on your shelf.

Suggestion: Play rhythm sticks to a steady beat.

DOWN THROUGH THE CHIMNEY
(Fingerplay)

Susan Ni

Down through the chimney, Santa slipped,
    (creep fingers downward)

Brushed off the dirt and snow that dripped,
    (brush clothes)

Looked 'round the room and then he crept
    (shade eyes, look around)   (tiptoe)

Right past the beds where the children slept.
              (rest head on hands)

Laid all the presents under the tree,
    (pantomime   (hands form pointed
laying presents)   tree above head)

Filled the stockings full for the children to see.
    (fill stockings)   (hand shade eyes)

Then tiptoed to the chimney and was out of sight,
    (tiptoe)   (swoop head from left to right)

'Til he jumped into his sleigh and flew off through the night.
    (jump)   (swoop arm upward)

INDEX